Emotional Healing
Workbook for Kids, and Teens

What is Emotional Healing?

Introduction

Have you ever gone through something scary or upsetting that still bothers you, even though it's in the past? Do you have nightmares, flashbacks, or often feel anxious, sad, or angry? If so, you're not alone. Many kids and teens experience difficult events that can affect their mental health.

This is where Emotional Healing can help. It's a type of therapy that assists in processing emotions, memories, and reactions to tough experiences, allowing you to feel better and move on with your life. In this guide, we'll explain what Emotional Healing is, how it works, and how it can help you feel better.

What is Emotional Healing?

Emotional Healing refers to therapeutic methods that help your brain process difficult experiences in a healthier way. When something scary or upsetting happens, your brain can sometimes get "stuck" on that memory, making it replay over and over again, even when you don't want it to. Emotional Healing techniques help your brain "unstick" the memory and process it in a way that feels less overwhelming and stressful.

What happens during an Emotional Healing session?

An Emotional Healing session typically begins with a conversation with your therapist about what's been bothering you and what you'd like to work on. You might start with some relaxation exercises to help you feel calm and secure. Then, your therapist will guide you to think about the upsetting memory while using various therapeutic techniques, such as visualization or breathing exercises.

You may also practice positive thinking or visualize comforting images to help you feel better. The session will wrap up with more relaxation exercises to help you feel grounded and safe. It's normal to feel tired or emotional afterward. Your therapist will help you understand your feelings and prepare for the next session.

How does Emotional Healing work?

Emotional Healing works a bit differently from other types of therapy because it involves moving your eyes back and forth while you think about the upsetting memory. Your therapist will guide you through this process in a safe and organized way. The eye movements can go side-to-side, up and down, or back and forth.

Sometimes, instead of eye movements, you might use other forms of stimulation, like tapping or listening to sounds that switch between your ears. These actions help your brain process the memory in a new way, making it feel less intense and easier to handle. Your therapist will also teach you skills and positive thoughts to help you feel more in control.

Is Emotional Healing right for me?

Emotional Healingcan be helpful for many kids and teens who have gone through tough experiences like abuse, accidents, bullying, or natural disasters. It's also useful for dealing with anxiety, depression, and other mental health struggles. However, Emotional Healing isn't the best option for everyone, so it's important to talk with your therapist to see if it's a good match for you. Your therapist will take time to carefully evaluate your situation to make sure Emotional Healing is safe and suitable for you before starting the therapy.

8 PHASES OF Emotional Healing

Emotional Healing

Is a type of therapy backed by research, commonly used to treat trauma and other mental health challenges. During the process, the therapist and client work together to focus on specific memories, emotions, and beliefs that are causing the client distress.

By working through these memories and changing negative thoughts into more positive ones, Emotional Healing helps people move past their traumatic experiences and improve their mental health and overall well-being.

1 — History & Treatment Planning
During this phase, the therapist gathers detailed information about the client's current problems and identifies specific areas that need to be worked on during therapy. This helps create a clear plan for treatment moving forward.

2 — Preparation
In this phase, the therapist teaches the client ways to calm down and manage stress. These coping skills and relaxation techniques will be helpful during the therapy sessions.

3 — Assessment
In this step, the therapist and client work together to figure out which memories, along with the emotions, beliefs, and feelings connected to them, are causing the most trouble.

4 — Desensitization
During this phase, the therapist uses techniques like eye movements, tapping, or sounds to help the client work through the specific memories and make the emotions connected to them feel less overwhelming.

5 — Installation
In this phase, the therapist works with the client to build up and reinforce positive thoughts and feelings that can take the place of the negative ones they've been experiencing.

6 — Body Scan
In this step, the therapist guides the client to notice if there are any remaining physical feelings or tension connected to the memories they've worked on during the session.

7 — Re-evaluation
At this stage, the therapist helps the client practice relaxation techniques to ensure they feel calm, stable, and grounded before the session ends.

8 — Closure
In this phase, the therapist reviews the client's progress and identifies any other areas that may need attention in future sessions.

CHOICE
I am not in control
Negative Thoughts

CHOICE
I have to be perfect/please everyone
Negative Thoughts

CHOICE
I am weak
Negative Thoughts

CHOICE
I am trapped
Negative Thoughts

CHOICE
I am in control
Positive Thoughts

CHOICE
I have power now
Positive Thoughts

CHOICE
I can help myselfl
Positive Thoughts

CHOICE
I have a way out
Positive Thoughts

POWER
I cannot succeed
Negative Thoughts

POWER
I cannot stand up for myself
Negative Thoughts

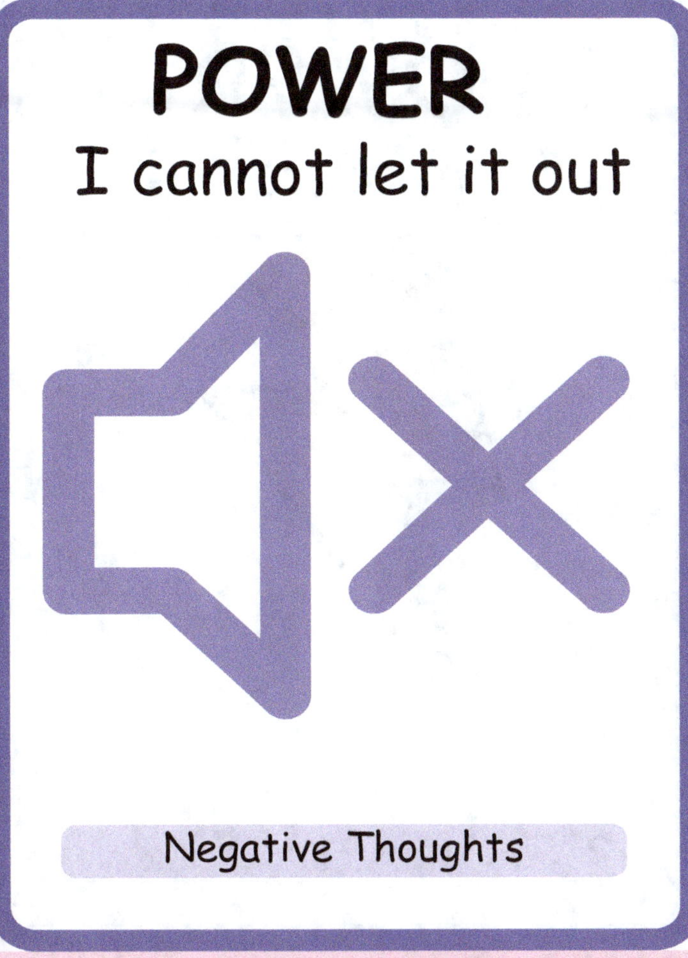

POWER
I cannot let it out
Negative Thoughts

POWER
I am powerless/helpless
Negative Thoughts

POWER
I can succeed

POWER
I can stand up for myself

POWER
I can let it out

POWER
I am powerful

VALUE
I am not good enough

Negative Thoughts

VALUE
I do not belong

Negative Thoughts

VALUE
I am permanently damaged

Negative Thoughts

VALUE
I am stupid

Negative Thoughts

VALUE
I am good enough

Positive Thoughts

VALUE
I can belong

Positive Thoughts

VALUE
I am restored

Positive Thoughts

VALUE
I am smart

Positive Thoughts

SAFETY
I cannot trust myself

Negative Thoughts

SAFETY
I cannot trust anyone

Negative Thoughts

SAFETY
I cannot show my emotions

Negative Thoughts

SAFETY
I am not safe

Negative Thoughts

SAFETY
I can trust myself
Trust
YOUR
Gut
Positive Thoughts

SAFETY
I can choose who to trust
Positive Thoughts

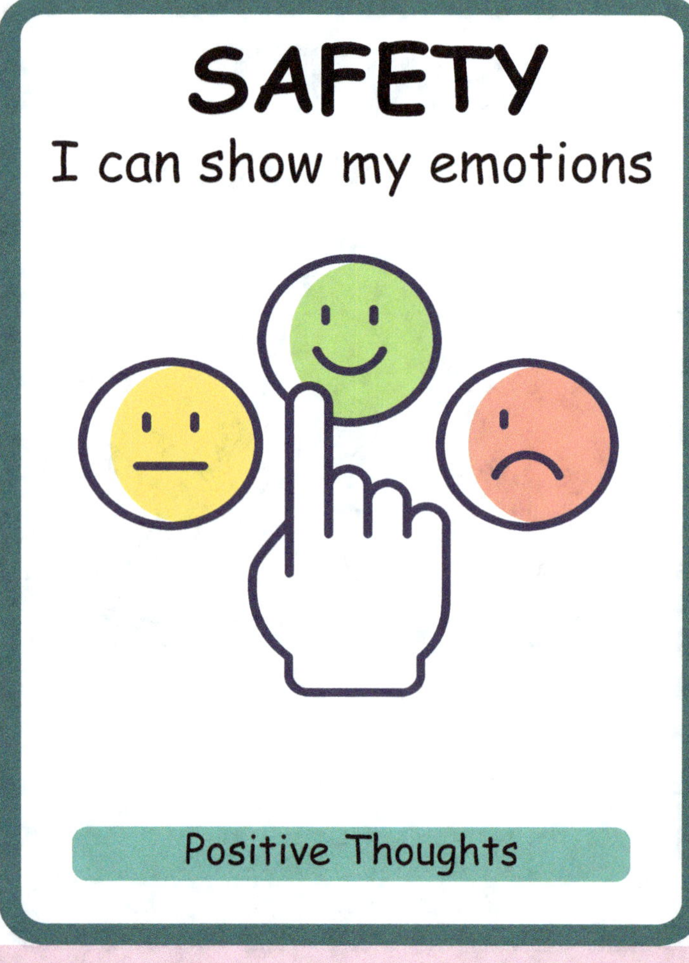
SAFETY
I can show my emotions
Positive Thoughts

SAFETY
I can create my sense of safety
THIS IS A
SAFE
SPACE
Positive Thoughts

RESPONSIBILITY
I should have known better

Negative Thoughts

RESPONSIBILITY
I did something wrong

RESPONSIBILITY
I should have done something

Negative Thoughts

RESPONSIBILITY
I am to blame

Negative Thoughts

RESPONSIBILITY
I did the best I could
Do your best
Positive Thoughts

RESPONSIBILITY
I did my best
Keep going
Positive Thoughts

RESPONSIBILITY
I do the best I can with what I have
Positive Thoughts

RESPONSIBILITY
I am not at fault
Positive Thoughts

T.I.C.E.S WORKSHEET

Notice what you are experiencing and briefly write it down using this log.

Trigger	Image	Thought/ Cognition	Emotion	Sensation	SUD Scale (0-10)	Coping Skill Used

BODY SENSATIONS

Our bodies can respond to stress in various physical ways. Below is a list of common sensations people might feel when they're stressed. Circle any that you experience, and feel free to add others if they aren't listed here.

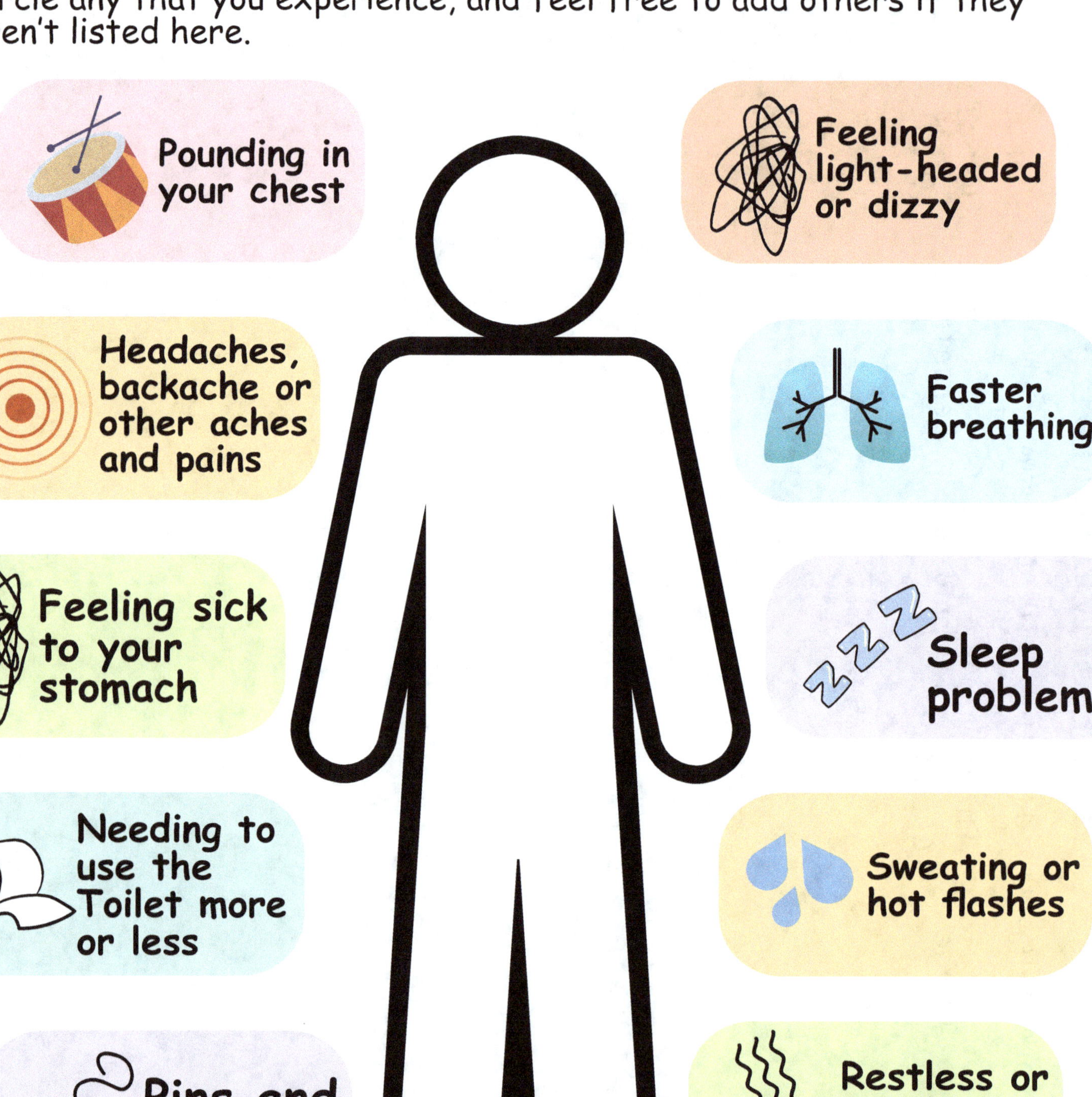

VALIDITY OF COGNITION SCALE (VOC)

A SUD, or **subjective unit of disturbance,** is used to determine the level of disturbance a memory holds. During a session, a memory is targeted by identifying each of the Memory components: image, cognition, affect andbody sensation.

The scale is set from 0-10 with 0 being no distress,and 10 being the most distressed.

10	Feelingout of control.
9	Extremely distressed.
8	Cannot concentrate.
7	Losing focus.
6	Moderate to strong anxiety.
5	Moderate anxiety.
4	Mild to moderate anxiety.
3	Mild anxiety; still functional.
2	Minimal anxiety.
1	Alert, focused; concentrating.
0	No distress; calm.

VALIDITY OF COGNITION SCALE (VOC)

The Validity of Cognition Scale (VOC), is used to determine if a belief about ourselves is true or not.

The scale is set from 1-7 with 1 being completely false, and 1 being completely true.

The longer the nose, the bigger the lie!

HOW TRUE DOES IT FEEL TO YOU?

SUDS TRACKER

Month:

WINDOW OF TOLERANCE

FIGHT-OR-FLIGHT
(Hyperarousal)

racing thoughts   out of control

panic

angry   yelling   too much energy

anxious   want to escape   fear

CALM
(Window of Tolerance)

feel in control   curious

"I got this"

safe   flexible thinking

"I can handle hard things"   present

FREEZE
(Hyperarousal)

low energy   too overwhelmed to move

sad   quiet   tired

shutting down   numb

WINDOW OF TOLERANCE

COPING SKILLS

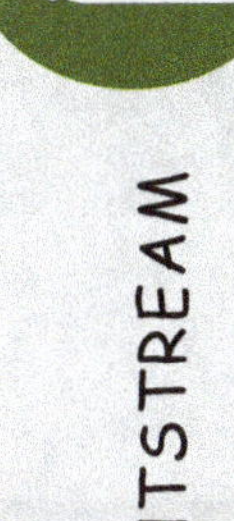

CALM YOUR SELF WITH A 5 FINGER BREATHING BRAIN BREAK

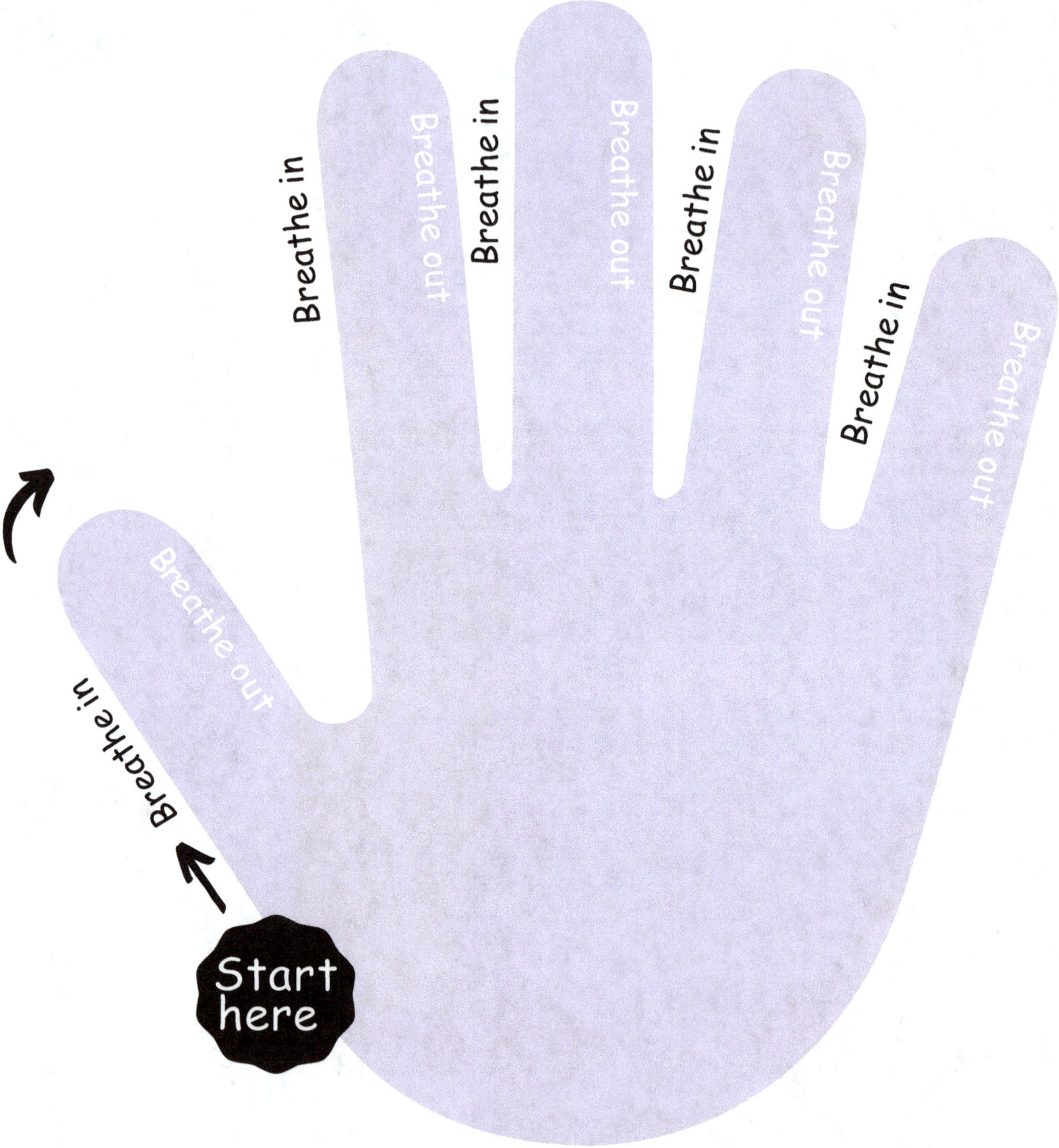

Gently trace around the edge of your hand using your index finger. Breathe in as you move up each finger, and breathe out as you move down. You can also try this breathing exercise with your own hand.

CALM YOUR SELF WITH A TRIANGLE BREATHING BRAIN BREAK

Begin at the bottom left corner of the triangle. Slowly trace your finger up one side while taking a deep breath in. As you move down the other side, hold your breath for three seconds. Breathe out as you trace along the bottom of the triangle. Keep repeating this until you feel calm.

CALM YOUR SELF WITH A SQUARE BREATHING BRAIN BREAK

Begin at the bottom left corner of the square. Move your finger up the side while taking a deep breath in. As you trace the second side, hold your breath for four seconds. Breathe out as you trace down the other side, and hold your breath again for four seconds as you move along the bottom of the square.

LAZY 8 BREATHING BRAIN BREAK

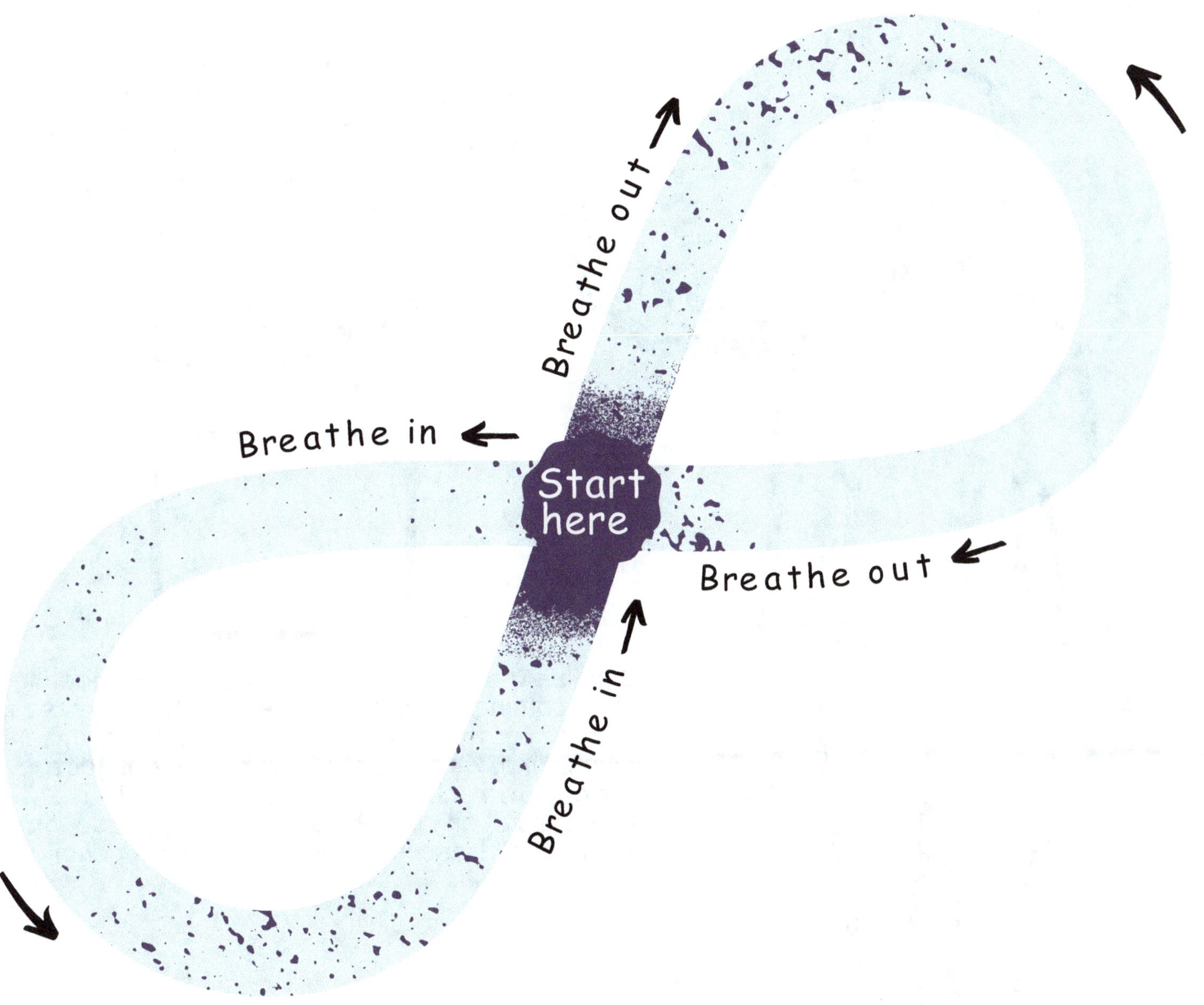

Place your finger at the center of the number 8. Slowly trace the left side of the 8 while breathing in. As you cross the middle, breathe out while tracing the right side.

Repeat this process until you feel calm and relaxed.

LIGHT STREAM

Close your eyes and focus on any uncomfortable sensations you might still feel in your body. Can you notice where in your body these feelings are right now?

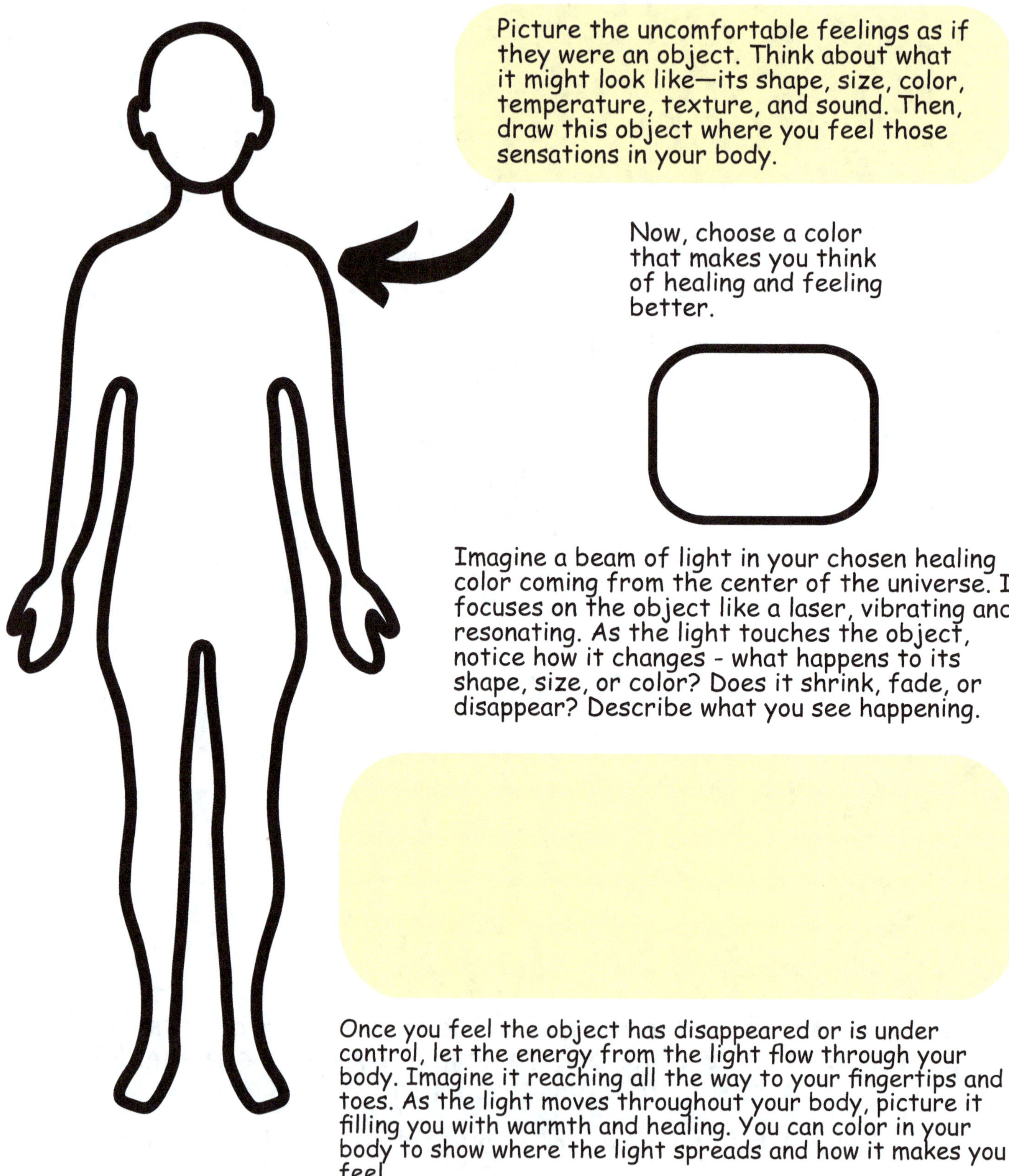

Picture the uncomfortable feelings as if they were an object. Think about what it might look like—its shape, size, color, temperature, texture, and sound. Then, draw this object where you feel those sensations in your body.

Now, choose a color that makes you think of healing and feeling better.

Imagine a beam of light in your chosen healing color coming from the center of the universe. It focuses on the object like a laser, vibrating and resonating. As the light touches the object, notice how it changes - what happens to its shape, size, or color? Does it shrink, fade, or disappear? Describe what you see happening.

Once you feel the object has disappeared or is under control, let the energy from the light flow through your body. Imagine it reaching all the way to your fingertips and toes. As the light moves throughout your body, picture it filling you with warmth and healing. You can color in your body to show where the light spreads and how it makes you feel.

SAFE PLACE

WHEN I AM HERE, I...

SEE:_____________________________

HEAR:_____________________________

FEEL:_____________________________

SMELL:_____________________________

TASTE:_____________________________

FEELING HAPPY

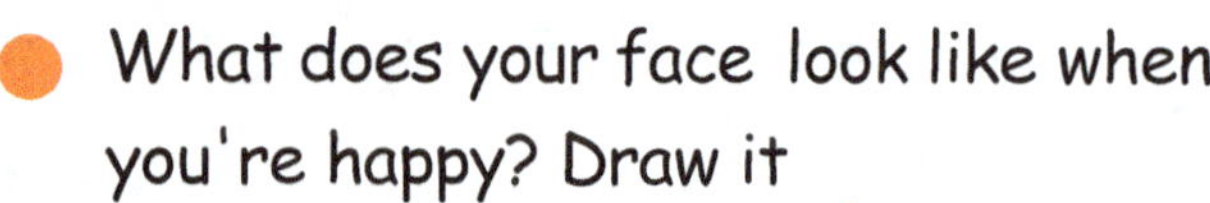

Happiness looks different for everyone.

- What does your face look like when you're happy? Draw it

- Write and draw 4 things that make you feel happy.

____

____

____

____

- Write and draw 4 ways in which you express that you are happy.

____

____

____

____

FEELING ANGRY

Anger looks different for everyone.

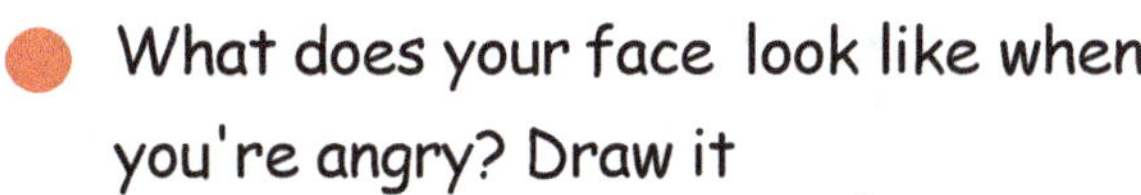

- What does your face look like when you're angry? Draw it

- Write and draw 4 things that make you feel angry.

____

____

____

____

- Write and draw 4 ways in which you express that you are angry.

____

____

____

____

FEELING SAD

Sadness looks different for everyone.

- What does your face look like when you're sad? Draw it

- Write and draw 4 things that make you feel sad.

____

____

____

____

- Write and draw 4 ways in which you express that you are sad.

____

____

____

____

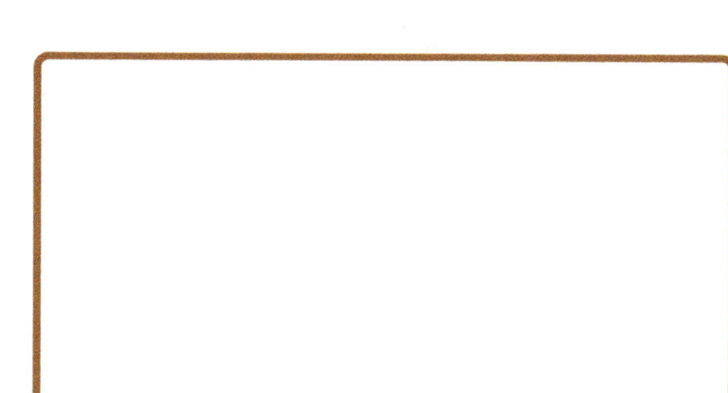

FEELING SCARED

Fear looks different for everyone.

- Write two synonymsof "scared"

____

- What does your face look like when you're scared? Draw it

- Write and draw 4 things that make you feel scared.

- Write and draw 4 ways in which you express that you are scared.

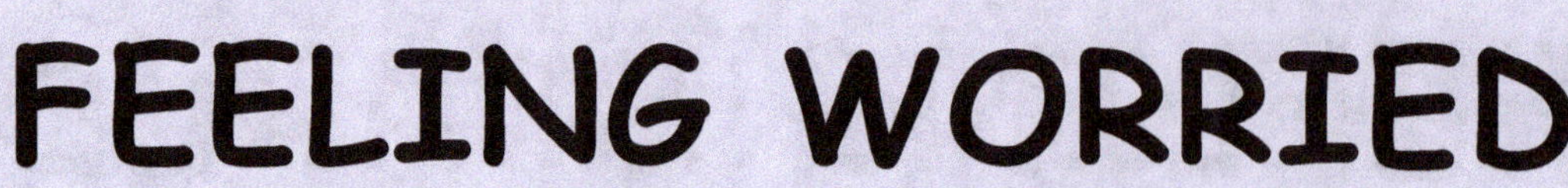

FEELING WORRIED

Worry looks different for everyone.

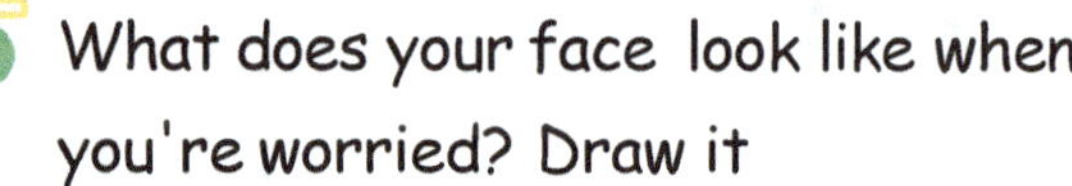

● What does your face look like when you're worried? Draw it

● Write and draw 4 things that make you feel worried.

● Write and draw 4 ways in which you express that you are worried.

____

____

____

____

Body Scan Exercise

Start by sitting comfortably with your back straight but relaxed, and both feet on the floor. You can also choose to stand or lie down with your head supported. Rest your hands in your lap or at your sides, and either close your eyes or keep them softly focused. Take a few slow, deep breaths, in through your nose or mouth, letting your belly expand as you breathe in and relax as you breathe out. Shift your focus from the outside world to what's happening inside your body, and return to your breath if you get distracted.

Now, focus on your feet, noticing any sensations there while breathing in and out. When you're ready, bring your attention up to your ankles, calves, knees, and thighs, paying attention to any feelings in your legs. If your mind drifts, gently bring your focus back to your legs without being hard on yourself. Let any discomfort or tightness just be there without fighting it.

As you exhale, move your attention to your lower back and hips, letting go of tension as you breathe. Gradually shift your focus up to your mid and upper back, noticing any tightness, warmth, or where your body touches your chair or bed. With each exhale, release any tension you're holding there.

Next, pay attention to your stomach and internal organs, noticing sensations like your clothes against your skin or digestion, without judging them. Move your focus to your chest and heart, feeling your heartbeat and how your chest rises and falls with each breath, letting go of any judgments.

Now, bring your focus to your hands and fingers, breathing into this area and noticing any sensations. If your mind drifts, just gently bring your focus back. On the next exhale, shift your attention to your arms, observing how they feel, and noticing any differences between your left and right arms. Allow the tension in your arms to soften and melt away.

Direct your attention to your neck, shoulders, and throat, areas where tension often builds. Notice any sensations, and let go of any thoughts or stories you may have about these areas. With each exhale, imagine the tension rolling off your shoulders.

Lastly, focus on your scalp, head, and face, noticing how the air moves through your nose or mouth, and allow any tightness to relax. Now, bring your awareness to your whole body, feeling the gentle rhythm of your breath moving through you.

At the end of the exercise, take one deep breath in, fully exhale, and open your eyes, bringing your awareness back to the present moment. Think about how this practice of awareness can help you feel more connected and calm throughout your day, and how it can positively impact those around you.

THE WORRY JAR

In this worksheet, you will imagine having a "worry jar" to help you handle negative emotions and memories. It's a fun way to put your worries aside for a while and feel more in control.

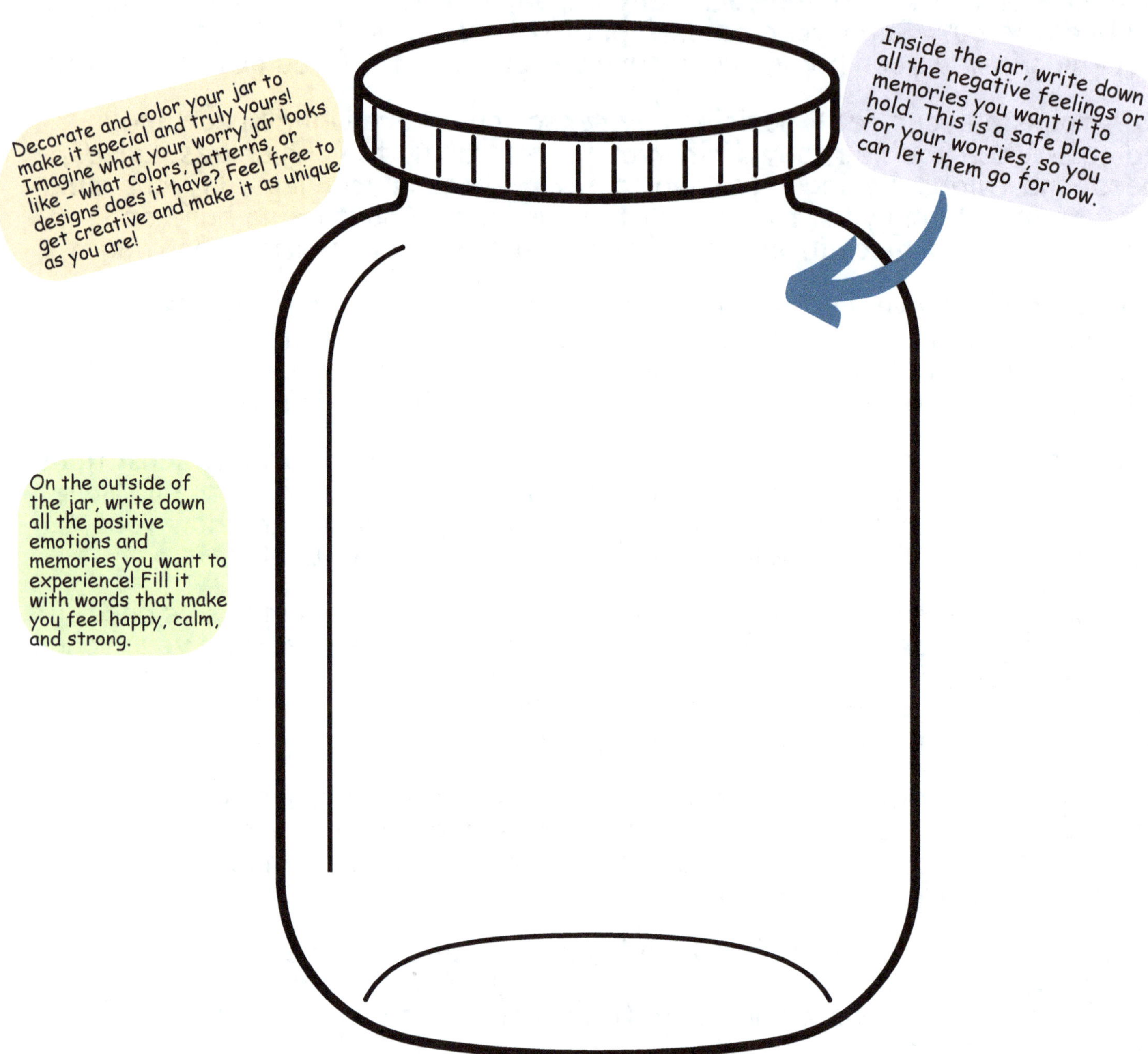

Now, think of a name for your worry jar that best represents it. Choose something that feels right, whether it's funny, comforting, or meaningful - something that matches what your jar means to you!

THE WORRY JAR PRACTICE

Think about some recent negative memories and how they make you feel. Now, imagine taking those memories and placing them inside your worry jar. How does it feel now that they're in the jar? Do you feel lighter, more in control, or calmer? Describe how putting those memories away changes the way you feel.

Now that your negative memories are safely stored in your jar, turn your attention to the positive memories and feelings that remain. How do these make you feel in your body? Do you feel warmth, lightness, or calmness? Take a moment to notice and describe the sensations these positive thoughts create.

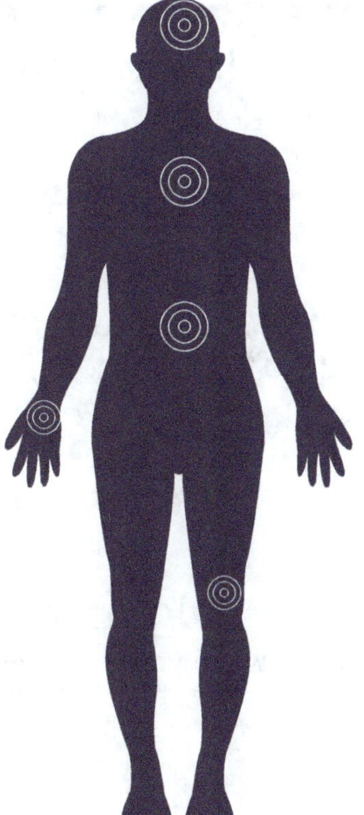

Emotional Healing CLIENT HISTORY

As you think about your recent situation, what emotions/feelings are you feeling right now?

Negative Core Belief

Based on your feelings/emotions above, what word(s) best describe your negative belief about yourself?

Touchstone Event

Think back when you felt those emotions/feelings/thoughts before. Write down the memory that comes to mind.

Was there an earlier event before the above event? If yes, describe what happened.

As a child, did you experience an event that triggered those same emotions/thoughts? If yes, describe what happened.

Positive Cognition

Think about when you experienced the worst/first event. Describe how you felt in the present tense. Next, reframe your negative thought with a positive alternative.

Emotional Healing CLIENT HISTORY

Future Desired Outcome

When you think about your problem, imagine how you'd like to handle it. Picture yourself being strong and confident as you face the situation. Describe in detail how you see yourself overcoming the challenge - what steps would you take, how would you feel, and what would change once you've dealt with it?

TARGETING SEQUENCE PLAN

Presenting Problem

First EMDR REPROCESSING SESSION TARGET:_______________________________
Touchstone Event

NC:____
PC:____

Past Incidents

AGE	INCIDENT

Present Triggers

Future Goals

Emotional Healing A-TIP

Step 7: POSITIVE BELIEF
How would you like to think about yourself in that situation?

☐ I accept who I am	☐ II can protect myself	☐ I overcame
☐ I am good enough	☐ I did enough	☐ I survived
☐ I am full of worth	☐ I am loveable	☐ I can control what I can
☐ I am okay	☐ I am safe now	☐ I am a good person
☐ I am adequate	☐ I did my best	☐ I have great worth

Step 8:
On a scale of 1-7 (where 1 is completely false, and 7 is completely true), how true do you think your positive thought above is now? ________________

Step 9:
Initiate eye movements, stop if any other memories or body sensations come up.

Do any other memories come up? Describe below:

Do you feel any body sensations? Describe below:

Emotional Healing A-TIP

Step 10: DESENSITIZE

Think about the incident and your negative thoughts. Follow my fingers. When I stop, think about the incident and tell me how disturbing it feels. We'll repeat this process as longs as your disturbances keep changing.

Round 1

1. BLS/DAS-5 to 10 round trip eye movements

2. Think about the incident now from 0-10: 0 is no disturbance and 10 is extreme disturbance:

☐ ☐ ☐ ☐ ☐ ☐ ☐ ☐ ☐ ☐
1 2 3 4 5 6 7 8 9 10

3. Take a deep breath. Think about the incident again. What do you notice?

Round 2

1. BLS/DAS-5 to 10 round trip eye movements

2. Think about the incident now from 0-10: 0 is no disturbance and 10 is extreme disturbance:

☐ ☐ ☐ ☐ ☐ ☐ ☐ ☐ ☐ ☐
1 2 3 4 5 6 7 8 9 10

3. Take a deep breath. Think about the incident again. What do you notice?

Round 3

1. BLS/DAS-5 to 10 round trip eye movements

2. Think about the incident now from 0-10: 0 is no disturbance and 10 is extreme disturbance:

☐ ☐ ☐ ☐ ☐ ☐ ☐ ☐ ☐ ☐
1 2 3 4 5 6 7 8 9 10

3. Take a deep breath. Think about the incident again. What do you notice?

Emotional Healing A-TIP

Step 10: DESENSITIZE
Think about the incident and your negative thoughts. Follow my fingers. When I stop, think about the incident and tell me how disturbing it feels. We'll repeat this process as longs as your disturbances keep changing.

Round
—

1. BLS/DAS-5 to 10 round trip eye movements

2. Think about the incident now from 0-10: 0 is no disturbance and 10 is extreme disturbance:

☐ ☐ ☐ ☐ ☐ ☐ ☐ ☐ ☐ ☐
1 2 3 4 5 6 7 8 9 10

3. Take a deep breath. Think about the incident again. What do you notice?

Round
—

1. BLS/DAS-5 to 10 round trip eye movements

2. Think about the incident now from 0-10: 0 is no disturbance and 10 is extreme disturbance:

☐ ☐ ☐ ☐ ☐ ☐ ☐ ☐ ☐ ☐
1 2 3 4 5 6 7 8 9 10

3. Take a deep breath. Think about the incident again. What do you notice?

Round
—

1. BLS/DAS-5 to 10 round trip eye movements

2. Think about the incident now from 0-10: 0 is no disturbance and 10 is extreme disturbance:

☐ ☐ ☐ ☐ ☐ ☐ ☐ ☐ ☐ ☐
1 2 3 4 5 6 7 8 9 10

3. Take a deep breath. Think about the incident again. What do you notice?

Emotional Healing A-TIP

Step 11: INSTALLATION AND ENHANCE VOC
Think about the incident and your positive thought. Does your positive thought still make sense, or is there a better positive thought? Describe below:

On a scale of 1-7, how true do you think your positive thought above is now? _____________

	1. BLS/DAS- 5 to 10 sets

Round 1

2. Think about the incident, how true does that thought feel now on a scale from 1-7, where 1 is completely false and 7 is completely true?

☐ ☐ ☐ ☐ ☐ ☐ ☐
1 2 3 4 5 6 7

1. BLS/DAS-5 to 10 round trip eye movements

Round 2

2. Think about the incident, how true does that thought feel now on a scale from 1-7, where 1 is completely false and 7 is completely true?

☐ ☐ ☐ ☐ ☐ ☐ ☐
1 2 3 4 5 6 7

1. BLS/DAS- 5 to 10 sets

Round 3

2. Think about the incident, how true does that thought feel now on a scale from 1-7, where 1 is completely false and 7 is completely true?

■ ☐ ■ ☐ ■ ☐ ■
1 2 3 4 5 6 7

1. BLS/DAS-5 to 10 round trip eye movements

Round 4

2. Think about the incident, how true does that thought feel now on a scale from 1-7, where 1 is completely false and 7 is completely true?

■ ☐ ■ ☐ ■ ☐ ■
1 2 3 4 5 6 7

Emotional Healing A-TIP

Step 10: DESENSITIZE
Think about the incident and your negative thoughts. Follow my fingers. When I stop, think about the incident and tell me how disturbing it feels. We'll repeat this process as longs as your disturbances keep changing.

Round 1

1. BLS/DAS-5 to 10 round trip eye movements

2. Think about the incident now from 0-10: 0 is no disturbance and 10 is extreme disturbance:

☐ ☐ ☐ ☐ ☐ ☐ ☐ ☐ ☐ ☐
1 2 3 4 5 6 7 8 9 10

3. Take a deep breath. Think about the incident again. What do you notice?

Round 2

1. BLS/DAS-5 to 10 round trip eye movements

2. Think about the incident now from 0-10: 0 is no disturbance and 10 is **extreme disturbance:**

☐ ☐ ☐ ☐ ☐ ☐ ☐ ☐ ☐ ☐
1 2 3 4 5 6 7 8 9 10

3. Take a deep breath. Think about the incident again. What do you notice?

Round 3

1. BLS/DAS-5 to 10 round trip eye movements

2. Think about the incident now from 0-10: 0 is no disturbance and 10 is extreme disturbance:

☐ ☐ ☐ ☐ ☐ ☐ ☐ ☐ ☐ ☐
1 2 3 4 5 6 7 8 9 10

3. Take a deep breath. Think about the incident again. What do you notice?

Emotional Healing A-TIP

Step 10: DESENSITIZE
Think about the incident and your negative thoughts. Follow my fingers. When I stop, think about the incident and tell me how disturbing it feels. We'll repeat this process as longs as your disturbances keep changing.

Round —

1. BLS/DAS-5 to 10 round trip eye movements

2. Think about the incident now from 0-10: 0 is no disturbance and 10 is extreme disturbance:

☐ ☐ ☐ ☐ ☐ ☐ ☐ ☐ ☐ ☐
1 2 3 4 5 6 7 8 9 10

3. Take a deep breath. Think about the incident again. What do you notice?

Round —

1. BLS/DAS-5 to 10 round trip eye movements

2. Think about the incident now from 0-10: 0 is no disturbance and 10 is extreme disturbance:

☐ ☐ ☐ ☐ ☐ ☐ ☐ ☐ ☐ ☐
1 2 3 4 5 6 7 8 9 10

3. Take a deep breath. Think about the incident again. What do you notice?

Round —

1. BLS/DAS-5 to 10 round trip eye movements

2. Think about the incident now from 0-10: 0 is no disturbance and 10 is extreme disturbance:

☐ ☐ ☐ ☐ ☐ ☐ ☐ ☐ ☐ ☐
1 2 3 4 5 6 7 8 9 10

3. Take a deep breath. Think about the incident again. What do you notice?

Emotional Healing A-TIP

Step 11: INSTALLATION AND ENHANCEVOC
Think about the incident and your positive thought. Doesyour positive thought still make sense,or is there a better positive thought? Describe below:

On a scale of 1-7, how true do you think your positive thought above is now? _____________

    1. BLS/DAS- 5 to 10 sets

Round 1

2. Think about the incident, how true does that thought feel now on a scale from 1-7, where 1 is completely false and 7 is completely true?

☐ ☐ ☐ ☐ ☐ ☐ ☐
1 2 3 4 5 6 7

    1.BLS/DAS-5 to 10 round trip eye movements

Round 2

2. Think about the incident, how true does that thought feel now on a scale from 1-7, where 1 is completely false and 7 is completely true?

☐ ☐ ☐ ☐ ☐ ☐ ☐
1 2 3 4 5 6 7

    1.BLS/DAS- 5 to 10 sets

Round 3

2. Think about the incident, how true does that thought feel now on a scale from 1-7, where 1 is completely false and 7 is completely true?

■ ■ ■ ■ ■ ■ ■
1 2 3 4 5 6 7

    1.BLS/DAS-5 to 10 round trip eye movements

Round 4

2. Think about the incident, how true does that thought feel now on a scale from 1-7, where 1 is completely false and 7 is completely true?

■ ■ ■ ■ ■ ■ ■
1 2 3 4 5 6 7

Emotional Healing A-TIP

Step 12: SESSIONCLOSE
Think about your experience today. Describe it below:

Emotional Healing A-TIP TREATMENT SUMMARY

Treatment Session: ☐ First   ☐ Reevaluation   ☐ Session #:_________________

Outcomes of Sesssion: ☐ Completed   ☐ Unfinished

Target Incident:

Irrational Belief:

Adaptive Belief:

Starting SUD:_______________________________Ending SUD:_______________________

Starting VOC:_______________________________Ending VOC:_______________________

Closure Intervention: ☐ None   ☐ Calm Place   ☐ Container   ☐ Eye-roll   ☐ Figure-eight
☐ Four-square

Client's current status: ☐ Unstable ☐ Stable   ☐ Excellent ☐ Other:_______________________

Treatment Notes:

Additional Interventions Planned (other than Emotional Healing/BLS):

Emotional Healing PROGRESS NOTE

Client ID:____   Age:_________________   Sex: ☐ M ☐ F

Treatment Session: ☐ First   ☐ Reevaluation   ☐ Session #:_________________

Prong being addressed: ☐ Past   ☐ Present   ☐ Future

Target of this session: ☐ Touchstone   ☐ Worst   ☐ Belief   ☐ Situation   ☐ Symptom

Type of BLS: ☐ Auditory   ☐ Eye Movements   ☐ Tactile   ☐ Combo   ☐ Other: _________

Target   Memory:____

Image:____

Emotions:____

Body Sensations:____

Negative Cognitions:____

Positive Cognitions:____

SUDS at Beginning of Session: SUDS at End of Session:

☐ ☐ ☐ ☐ ☐ ☐ ☐ ☐ ☐ ☐ ☐   ☐ ☐ ☐ ☐ ☐ ☐ ☐ ☐ ☐ ☐ ☐
0 1 2 3 4 5 6 7 8 9 10   0 1 2 3 4 5 6 7 8 9 10

VOC at Begining:

☐ ☐ ☐ ☐ ☐ ☐ ☐
1 2 3 4 5 6 7

Positive Cognition Installed: ☐ YES ☐ NO   Notes:_________________________________

Outcome of Session: ☐ Completed   ☐ Unfinished

Stabilization intervention: ☐ Breathing   ☐ Container   ☐ Calm Place   ☐ Body Scan
☐ Lightstream

Client Status: ☐ Unstable   ☐ Stable   ☐ Other:_________________________________

Treatment Notes:

Additional Interventions Planned (other than Emotional Healing/BLS):

Congratulations on finishing the Emotional Healing Workbook for Kids and Teens!

You've taken an important step in understanding and managing your emotions. Remember, you have the strength and tools inside you to handle tough memories and feelings. Every time you practice what you've learned, you're getting stronger, calmer, and more in control. Healing takes time, but you're on the right path, and you don't have to do it alone – there are always people who can help. Keep believing in yourself, and know that you're capable of overcoming any challenge that comes your way!

www.ingramcontent.com/pod-product-compliance
Lightning Source LLC
LaVergne TN
LVHW060300200726
843507LV00009B/1160